Karen's Wedding

Look for these
and other books about Karen
in the
Baby-sitters Little Sister series:

1 Karen's Witch
2 Karen's Roller Skates
3 Karen's Worst Day
4 Karen's Kittycat Club
5 Karen's School Picture
6 Karen's Little Sister
7 Karen's Birthday
8 Karen's Haircut
9 Karen's Sleepover
#10 Karen's Grandmothers
#11 Karen's Prize
#12 Karen's Ghost
#13 Karen's Surprise
#14 Karen's New Year
#15 Karen's in Love
#16 Karen's Goldfish
#17 Karen's Brothers
#18 Karen's Home Run
#19 Karen's Good-bye
#20 Karen's Carnival
#21 Karen's New Teacher
#22 Karen's Little Witch
#23 Karen's Doll
#24 Karen's School Trip
#25 Karen's Pen Pal

#26 Karen's Ducklings
#27 Karen's Big Joke
#28 Karen's Tea Party
#29 Karen's Cartwheel
#30 Karen's Kittens
#31 Karen's Bully
#32 Karen's Pumpkin Patch
#33 Karen's Secret
#34 Karen's Snow Day
#35 Karen's Doll Hospital
#36 Karen's New Friend
#37 Karen's Tuba
#38 Karen's Big Lie
#39 Karen's Wedding
#40 Karen's Newspaper

Super Specials:
1 Karen's Wish
2 Karen's Plane Trip
3 Karen's Mystery
4 Karen, Hannie, and
     Nancy: The Three
     Musketeers
5 Karen's Baby

Little Sister

Karen's Wedding

Ann M. Martin

Illustrations by Susan Tang

A
LITTLE APPLE
PAPERBACK

SCHOLASTIC INC.
New York Toronto London Auckland Sydney

ISBN 0-590-45654-7

12 11 10 9 8 7 6 5 4 3   5 6 7 8/9

Printed in the U.S.A.   40

First Scholastic printing, June 1993

For the Monagles,
Ed and Peggy,
Maureen, Michael, and John

The Flower Girl

Hello, it's me again. Karen Brewer, remember? I am seven years old. I am in Ms. Colman's second grade class. I go to Stoneybrook Academy in Stoneybrook, Connecticut. In one month, something gigundoly exciting is going to happen. My teacher is going to get married. Guess who is going to be her flower girl? Me! My mother and stepfather are very good friends of Ms. Colman and Mr. Simmons. (Mr. Simmons is Ms. Colman's fiancé. He is the man she is going to marry.) I cannot wait to be a flower girl. I just love getting dressed up.

I love my teacher, too. And I love school. I am very lucky because my two best friends are also in Ms. Colman's room. They are Nancy Dawes and Hannie Papadakis.

Here are some facts about my classroom:

We have a class pet. He is a guinea pig named Hootie.

We have a class bully. He is a boy named Bobby Gianelli. Once, Bobby and I almost got into a fistfight, but Mrs. Gianelli stopped us. Unfortunately, Bobby lives right down the street from my mother's house.

My husband is in the classroom. He is a boy named Ricky Torres. Ricky and I used to be enemies, but then we got married. We got married on the playground one afternoon. (Of course, Ricky is not *really* my husband.)

The kids who wear glasses have to sit in the front row. This is Ms. Colman's rule. (She wears glasses herself.) These people are the glasses-wearers: Natalie Springer, Ricky, me. I love Ms. Colman, but I do not like her rule. Before I got glasses, I sat in the back row with Nancy and Hannie. But then I had to move.

One Monday morning, Hannie and Nancy and I were sitting on some desks in the back of the classroom. School had not started yet. Ms. Colman was not even in the room. My friends and I were talking. (We call ourselves the Three Musketeers because we spend so much time together.)

"Hi, you guys," said a shy voice.

I looked up. There was Natalie Springer. Natalie is not too sure of herself. She speaks quietly. (Also, she lisps. She goes to speech class three times a week.) Her socks are always falling down. She makes mistakes and then she feels bad. Sometimes she does not pay attention. She is a WORRIER. But she can be a very good friend.

"Hi, Natalie," my friends and I replied.

"I have an idea," Natalie told us. "I think

we should give Ms. Colman and Mr. Simmons a wedding present. From our whole class."

"We already did," I said. "We played the special song."

In school, my classmates and I had learned to play instruments. One of the music teachers, Mrs. Dade, taught us to play as a band. At the end of the band unit, we put on a concert. As a surprise, we learned how to play "Here Comes the Bride" for Ms. Colman. Even Mrs. Dade did not know we were teaching ourselves that song. Ms. Colman just loved her surprise. She even cried a little.

"I know," said Natalie. "And the song was nice. But that was before Ms. Colman invited us all to her wedding. Now we really should buy a present for Ms. Colman and Mr. Simmons. Something they can open."

I looked at Nancy and Hannie. My friends and I nodded our heads. Natalie was right. If we were going to the wedding,

4

we should buy a present. When Mommy and Seth were married they got lots of presents. When Daddy and Elizabeth were married, they got lots of presents, too. I am sort of an expert on weddings.

2

Other Weddings

I have had some experience at being a flower girl. I was the flower girl in Daddy's wedding, when he married Elizabeth. (Elizabeth is my stepmother.)

This is the interesting thing about my parents: First they got divorced, then they each got married again. See, a long time ago, when I was just a little kid, I had a regular family. I lived in a big house with Mommy and Daddy and my little brother Andrew. (Andrew is four now, going on five.) But Mommy and Daddy were not happy. They began to fight a lot. Finally, they said they were getting divorced. Mommy moved out of the big house. She moved to a little house. She took Andrew and me with her. (Daddy stayed in the big house. He grew up there.)

After awhile Mommy met Seth and they got married. And Daddy met Elizabeth, and *they* got married. So now I have two families right here in Stoneybrook, one in the little house, one in the big house. Andrew and I live in the big house every other weekend, and on some vacations. The rest of the time we live at the little house.

This is the little-house family: Mommy, Seth, Andrew, me, Rocky, Midgie, Emily Junior. Rocky and Midgie are Seth's cat and dog. Emily Junior is my rat.

This is my big-house family: Daddy, Elizabeth, Kristy, Charlie, Sam, David Michael, Emily Michelle, Nannie, Andrew, me, Boo-Boo, Shannon, Goldfishie, and Crystal Light the Second. Kristy, Charlie, Sam, and David Michael are Elizabeth's kids, so they are my stepsister and stepbrothers. Kristy is thirteen. I love her. She is the best, best big sister. And she is an extra good baby-sitter. Charlie and Sam are in high school. David Michael is seven like me. (But he goes to a different school.) Emily Michelle is my adopted sister. She is two and a half. Daddy and Elizabeth adopted her from a faraway country called Vietnam. (I named my rat after Emily.) Nannie is Elizabeth's mother. That makes her my stepgrand-mother. Nannie helps to take care of us kids. Let me see. Boo-Boo, Shannon, Gold-fishie, and Crystal Light the Second are pets. Boo-Boo is Daddy's cross old tomcat. Shannon is David Michael's puppy. Gold-fishie and Crystal Light are (what else?) goldfish. They belong to Andrew and me. Isn't it a good thing the big house is so big?

I have special nicknames for my brother and me. I call us Andrew Two-Two and Karen Two-Two. This is because we have two of so many things. We have two houses and two families, two mommies and two daddies, two cats and two dogs. I have two bicycles, one at each house. I have two stuffed cats, exactly alike. Moosie stays at the big house, Goosie stays at the little house. And Andrew and I both have books and toys and clothes at each house. I also have my two best friends. Nancy lives next door to Mommy. Hannie lives across the street from Daddy, and one house down.

Andrew and I do not have two of *every-thing*, though. For instance, I have only one pair of roller skates. I have to remember to bring them back and forth between the little house and the big house. Another thing I do not like about being a two-two is that when I am at the little house, I miss my big-house family. And when I am at the big house, I miss my little-house family.

Still, having two families is fun. Being in my parents' weddings was fun, too. That was why I was looking forward to being in Ms. Colman's wedding. (Of course, I was looking forward to getting a new, beautiful flower girl's dress, too.)

3

At Ms. Colman's House

I am so, so lucky that Mommy and Seth have become good friends with Ms. Colman and Mr. Simmons. They eat dinner together often. Ms. Colman and Mr. Simmons come over to our house about once a week. So I get to see my teacher even when I am not in school. Plus, I was going to be in their wedding, of course. But do you know what? I had never been to Ms. Colman's house. Not until one afternoon when Mommy said to Andrew and me, "Finish up your snacks, kids. I want to get going."

I had just come home from school. Andrew had been home from preschool for several hours, but he likes to have a snack with me when I get home.

"Where are we going?" I asked Mommy. (You never know what could be in store.)

Mommy smiled. "We are going to Ms. Colman's house," she replied.

"We *are*? Yes!" I cried. I had just left my teacher, and now I would get to see her again. More importantly, I would get to see the inside of her house.

Ms. Colman does not live in Stoneybrook. She lives away from town, out in the country. We drove by pastures and cows and horses and sheep and farmhouses before we came to Ms. Colman's driveway. I liked her house right away. It is exactly the same size as the little house. It is surrounded by woods. It looks cozy.

We stood on Ms. Colman's porch. Mommy lifted Andrew up so he could ring the doorbell. *Bong-bong.*

"Hello!" called Ms. Colman as she let us inside.

First the adults had to talk for awhile. Mommy and Seth are giving a party for Ms. Colman and Mr. Simmons a week before the wedding. See, neither my teacher nor Mr. Simmons has much family. And they do not have any family that lives right nearby. Ms. Colman's mother lives in Chicago. Her sister and her sister's husband and their daughter live all the way across the country in the state of Oregon. They cannot even come to the wedding. Ms. Colman is sad about that. She loves her sister. And she had hoped her niece would be her flower girl. (It is a good thing she has me, since I am an expert flower girl.)

Anyway, there was no family to give a party for the bride and groom. So Mommy and Seth said, "We would like to do that. The party will be our wedding present to you."

Now Mommy and Ms. Colman were talking about the party. They were making lists:

a list of friends to invite, a list of foods to serve, a list of things to buy or borrow.

Andrew and I grew bored. We wandered around the house. We looked at Ms. Colman's things. She had lots of photos. Many of them were pictures of a girl about my age.

"Who's this?" I asked Ms. Colman. I pointed to one of the photographs.

"That's my niece," she replied. "My sister's daughter in Oregon. Her name is Caroline. She is seven like you." Ms. Colman paused and smiled. "She likes to ride horses and play the piano. She is very quiet and sweet. I have not seen her in almost a year, though. I miss her."

"It is too bad she cannot come to the wedding," I said.

Ms. Colman nodded. "I know. But it is too big a trip for her family to take just now."

Mommy and my teacher finished writing their lists. Then Mommy said, "All right, let's talk about the dress Karen will wear."

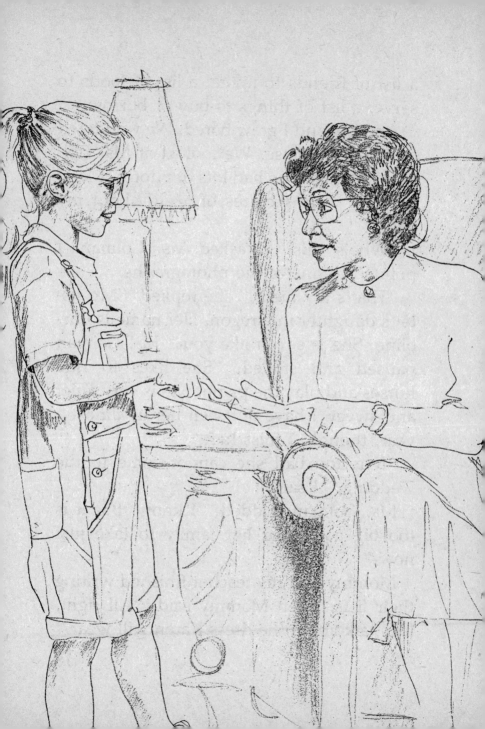

"The bridesmaids' dresses will be pale blue," said Ms. Colman, "so I think Karen's should be, too. But it does not need to be long."

"We should go shopping soon," said Mommy.

We decided to go the following week. A shopping trip with my teacher.

4

Presents

Nancy and Hannie and Natalie and I were sitting on the desks in the back of our classroom. It was another early morning. School had not started yet. Ms. Colman had not even arrived.

"We should talk about Ms. Colman's present," said Natalie.

"We need the other kids," I told her. "Hey, Ricky! Addie! Come here! Terri, Tammy, Hank! Everybody!"

My classmates gathered around us. By now, Natalie had told us her idea. And we all wanted to help buy a present. (Natalie was very pleased that we liked her idea so much.) But we had not talked about *what* to buy. None of us had bought a wedding present before.

"I think the present should be fancy," said Natalie. "Wedding presents are usually fancy. Like gold or silver."

"Or else they are big," added Ricky. "They come in big boxes. Toasters and blenders and things like that. Big things for the kitchen."

"When my cousin got married," said Addie Sidney, "she got sixteen toasters. She had to return fifteen of them."

"Maybe we should not get a toaster," said Ricky.

"How many blenders did your cousin get?" asked Nancy.

"Just four," Addie replied.

"Maybe we should not get a blender either," said Ricky.

"How about a clock?" said Pamela Harding.

"Is that a good wedding present?" asked Nancy.

Pamela shrugged.

"Maybe some plates," said Addie. "My cousin got these dessert plates and she really liked them. At least she said she would keep them."

"Ms. Colman has plates," I told my friends. "I saw them in her house." (I liked being able to remind people that I had been *inside* my teacher's house.) "She has plenty of plates," I added.

"What would be really fancy?" wondered Natalie.

"A clock?" suggested Pamela again.

"She has two," I announced. "I saw — "

"I know, I know. You saw them in her house," said Pamela crossly.

"Well, I did!"

"Hey!" called Hank Reubens from the doorway. "Ms. Colman is coming!"

"Secret meeting on the playground today!" I cried. Then we ran for our desks.

18

We were sitting quietly by the time Ms. Colman entered the room.

After lunch, my friends and I met by the monkey bars on the playground.

"I have an idea about our present," I said. "Maybe my big brother could take some of us shopping one day. Charlie could drive us downtown in the Junk Bucket." (The Junk Bucket is his rattly old car.) "And maybe Kristy could come, too. She could give us shopping advice."

"I wonder how much a present will cost," said Natalie.

"I wonder how much money we have," I said.

"I have two dollars!" called Hank.

"I have a dollar and eighty cents," said Leslie Morris.

"Wait, wait. Someone should add this up," I said.

"I will," replied Hannie. "Everybody, tell me how much money you have."

Hannie wrote the numbers on a piece of

notebook paper. She wrote them in a long column. She took forever adding them up. When she was finally finished, she said, "We have nineteen dollars and eleven cents. I think. That is not very much."

It certainly wasn't. It was not enough for a fancy wedding present.

5

Shopping

I talked to Charlie. I talked to Kristy. They said they would help my friends and me look for a wedding present. They said they would take Nancy, Hannie, Natalie, and me downtown on Saturday.

We met at the big house.

Charlie sat behind the wheel of the Junk Bucket. The rest of us slid in after him. I sat in front between Charlie and Kristy. My friends sat in back.

"Seat belts!" called Charlie. We buckled up.

"Where do you want to go first?" Kristy asked me.

I turned around to look at my friends.

"The jewelry store," answered Natalie. "They have silver stuff."

Boy, did they ever.

"This costs more than two thousand dollars!" squeaked Hannie. We were standing in the store. She was looking at a silver bowl.

"These candlesticks cost eight hundred dollars!" cried Nancy.

"Maybe this was not a good idea," said Natalie softly. "Maybe we cannot buy Ms. Colman a present. I did not know grownups pay so much money for wedding gifts."

"They don't," said Kristy. "Not always. Come on, let's look somewhere else. We do not have to get the present here."

Next we went to a gift store.

"Here is a china picture frame," I said. "It only costs nine dollars. We could buy it and have money left over."

"Not special enough," said Natalie.

"Here is a beautiful pen for twenty-four dollars," said Nancy.

"Too boring," said Natalie.

"Here is something not boring," said Hannie. "It is so not boring I do not even know what it is."

"Too weird," said Natalie.

We left the gift store.

"Now what?" said Charlie.

I looked at Natalie. I thought she was going to cry.

"We have not seen a single good thing," she wailed.

"I have an idea," said Kristy. "Let's go to Bellair's."

"The department store?" I asked.

Kristy nodded. "We will go to the Fine Gifts counter. You will see lots of pretty things that do not cost too much and do not cost too little. I have bought all kinds of presents there."

So Charlie drove to Bellair's, and Kristy led the way to Fine Gifts.

We looked and looked and looked. But

we did not see the perfect gift. Not at first. Then a salesman asked if he could help us.

Kristy told him what we were shopping for.

The man frowned. Then he said, "How about this?" He held up a very beautiful silver cup.

"Ms. Colman could put it on her desk," said Nancy.

"She could keep her pencils in it!" exclaimed Natalie.

"You could have it engraved," added the man. "We could write your teacher's name on it. Or anything else you want."

My friends and I looked at each other. We smiled. Then I said, "How much is it?"

The man told us the price. With the engraving the cup would cost more than sixty dollars.

"Well," said Natalie, "I guess we could raise some money."

We had to leave the cup behind in the store. We hoped that the next time we came back, we would be able to buy it.

6

Secrets

"Secret meeting on the playground. Pass it on," I whispered to Ricky.

"Secret meeting on the playground. Pass it on," Ricky whispered to Bobby.

It was Monday morning. Our shopping trip was over and we had found the perfect wedding gift for our teacher. But we needed to earn a lot of money before we could buy it. So my classmates and I needed to hold another secret meeting on the playground. We had to be able to talk when Ms. Colman was not around. The playground is a good place for that, unless our teacher has playground duty. But Ms. Colman was not on duty that week. So we planned a secret meeting.

We met at the monkey bars after lunch. This is a good meeting place for everyone except Addie Sidney. Addie uses a wheelchair. She needs some help getting from the cafeteria to the monkey bars across the playground. But once she's there, she is fine. And the rest of us can sit on the grass or climb around on the bars.

"Okay, everybody," I said when my class was ready for the meeting. "Natalie and Nancy and Hannie and I went shopping on Saturday."

"Shopping for the wedding present," added Natalie.

"Did you buy anything?" asked Pamela.

"Not yet," I replied.

"But we found the perfect gift," said Hannie.

"And it is fancy," said Natalie.

"Is it gold or silver?" asked Leslie.

"Silver," Natalie answered proudly. "A silver cup."

"A cup?" repeated Leslie. "Is that all?"

"Well . . ." said Natalie. Her chin began to quiver.

"We looked at a bowl," I told Leslie. "It cost two thousand dollars."

"Oh," said Leslie.

"The cup is perfect," spoke up Nancy. "Ms. Colman can keep it on her desk and put her pencils in it. Plus, we can have the cup engraved."

"Is it very expensive?" asked Addie.

"We will have to earn about forty more dollars," I told her.

"I guess we can do that," she said.

"Let's vote on the cup," said Hannie. "Who here thinks we should buy the silver cup for Ms. Colman's wedding present?"

Guess what. Every single kid in our class raised his or her hand.

Natalie grinned. "I guess the cup was a good idea after all," she said.

"Right," I agreed. "Now all we have to do is earn forty dollars."

"Forty dollars," repeated Hank with a sigh.

"Well, that is not really *so* much," said Hannie. "If each of us earns two or three dollars, we will have enough."

"When we add it to the money we already have," I said. "Do not forget that. We have to be sure not to spend our money."

"How will we earn more money?" asked Tammy.

"Have a bake sale!" cried Pamela. "We could hold it downtown."

"No!" I shrieked. "We cannot do that. Ms. Colman might find out about it. Then the surprise would be ruined. We have to do littler things."

"Odd jobs?" suggested Bobby.

"Perfect," I replied. I glanced at Hannie and Nancy. We smiled at each other. I knew we were thinking the same thing. Once, we wanted to earn money to buy

three special dolls we call the Doll Sisters.
So we started an odd-job service. Now we
could run our service again. We could walk
dogs and weed gardens and clean stuff.

We were going to be very busy.

7

The Perfect Dress

On Tuesday, I got to see Ms. Colman after school again. It was time to go shopping for my flower girl dress.

"Where are we going shopping?" I asked. "In the department store?"

"No," said Mommy. "I thought we would go to Washington Mall. We will be able to look in lots of stores there."

"Oh, boy," groaned Andrew. "This is going to be really boring. I can tell."

Andrew just hates shopping for clothes. He would rather wear raggedy, holey old things forever than buy one new pair of jeans.

"Sorry," Mommy said to my brother. "We are going anyway. It will just take a couple of hours. Bring a book with you."

We piled into the car and drove to the mall. We picked up Ms. Colman on the way.

As soon as we walked inside the mall, Andrew said, "May I have some chocolate chip cookies, please?"

And I said, "May I have an Orange Julius?"

"One treat for each of you," Mommy answered. "That is all."

When we had finished our treats we went into Karen's Boutique.

"I am sure we will find something here," I said. "The store is named after me."

But we did not see anything that was just right.

"Let's look in the Finery Shoppe," said Ms. Colman.

I tried on a blue flowered dress. It was too tight.

I tried on a dress with a long sash and a wide white collar.

"Beautiful," Ms. Colman said.

"It itches," I said.

"I'm bored," Andrew said.

"I'm sorry," Mommy said.

We went to Tiger Lily's. I found a gorgeous purple and orange dress with layers of lace and ruffles. *"Please* may I try it on?" I begged.

"It is the wrong color," said Ms. Colman.

"Luckily," whispered Mommy.

We went to the Nutcracker. I was the one who spotted a blue dress that was not too plain and not too fancy. It was just my size, too. I tried it on. I twirled around in it.

"Lovely," said Mommy.

"Perfect," said Ms. Colman.

"I'm boreder than before," said Andrew.

We bought the dress and a straw hat and a pair of white gloves. I was ready to be a flower girl.

8

The Long Saturday

It was Saturday morning. And it was a big-house weekend. Andrew and I were at Daddy's. Guess what I was doing that Saturday. I was working. My classmates and I had decided to spend the day earning money for Ms. Colman's wedding present. Hannie and Nancy and I had been telling people about our odd-job service.

Daddy was the first person to hire me. "I need someone to cut the dead flowers off the rosebushes. Can you do the job?"

I nodded my head. "Yes," I told him

firmly. "I have done that before. I know exactly how to do the job."

Snip, snip, snippety-snip. I wore a pair of gloves. I used the gardening shears. I was very careful. Daddy paid me fifty cents.

The next person who hired me was Elizabeth. "Can you please watch Emily for half an hour? She wants to play in the yard, but I will be busy indoors. I will pay you fifty cents."

"Sure," I said.

I played horsie with Emily in the front yard. I kept her away from the road. Across the street I could see Hannie. She was giving Noodle the poodle a bath.

"This is my first job!" Hannie called to me. "When Noodle is clean, I am going to wash the windows on our porch!"

"I am working, too!" I shouted back. "I have earned fifty cents!"

Emily and I played in the yard for half an hour. I collected my money. I had earned one whole dollar for Ms. Colman's present.

At lunchtime the phone rang. "Hi, Karen. It's me," said Nancy. Nancy was calling to tell me she had earned seventy-five cents. "And Natalie called me," she added. "She and the twins are running a lemonade stand on their street. They have earned a dollar and a quarter."

All afternoon, my friends and I called each other. We were working hard. It was a long Saturday.

Bobby Gianelli watched his sister Alicia.

Pamela Harding cleaned out her room and sold all her junk to her neighbors. (I could not imagine wanting to buy Pamela's junk.)

Addie Sidney read stories to her neighbor, who was not feeling well.

Hank Reubens walked up and down his street and picked up bottles and cans. Then he returned them to the grocery store for a deposit. (He earned thirty-five cents.)

At five o'clock on Saturday afternoon, Ricky telephoned me. "I feel like I have been working forever," he said. "And I have only earned a dollar and a quarter. That is not very much."

"Hank only earned thirty-five cents," I told him.

"What are we going to do? We are not earning enough money."

"Well," I said slowly, "we still have a few more weeks."

"We could earn the money faster if we could do one big project," said Ricky. "All of us together. I think we should do that."

"But what if Ms. Colman finds out?"

"I don't know. I guess we do not have to tell her what the money is for."

So Ricky and I thought and thought. We talked to Natalie. We talked to Hank and Nancy and Hannie. Finally we decided to hold a car wash. We would have it at Hank's house. He lives downtown, so lots of cars drive up and down his street. His parents said we could run the car wash the very next day. And Sam and Charlie and

Kristy said they would help us. So did our classmates.

"We just have to hope Ms. Colman will not be in Stoneybrook tomorrow," I said to Ricky. "We have to hope she will not see us."

9

Hank's Car Wash

This is what you need for a car wash: hoses and buckets and sponges and soap and water and rags and maybe some wax and a car vacuum.

"I know something else you need," said Ricky. "Cars."

It was Sunday morning. Charlie had driven me to Hank's house. Sam and Kristy had come along. At Hank's, we had met Ricky and Natalie. My friends and I had made a big sign. It said:

GET YOUR CAR WASHED HERE!
ONLY $2.00!
FAST SERVICE — EXPERT WORK!

(Kristy had helped us figure out what to put on the sign.)

Then we had found the hoses and buckets and sponges and things. We had connected the hoses. We had made sure the sprayer worked. We were ready to go. But we did not have any customers. Not one.

Sam looked at his watch. "Well, it is still early," he said.

"I know how to get customers," I announced. I ran to the sidewalk. I shrieked, *"Come get your car wa — "*

Kristy clapped her hand over my mouth. "Shh, Karen!" she said. "You could wake up the dead."

"But we need customers."

"Here comes a car!" called Hank.

A station wagon was driving down the street. It stopped by our sign. The door opened and Pamela climbed out.

"Oh, it is only Pamela," I said.

But Pamela's father wanted to have his car washed. He was our very first customer. My friends and I set to work. We soaped and rinsed and polished. When we had finished, the car gleamed.

"Beautiful," said Mr. Harding. And he paid us *three* dollars.

As soon as Mr. Harding had left, another car pulled up by the sign. A woman climbed out. "Boy, am I glad to find you," she said. "My car is filthy. It needs a bath badly."

Hank adjusted his baseball cap. "Glad to be of service," he said.

We washed the car and earned two more dollars.

When the woman had left, Terri and Tammy came by to help. Ricky said he had to leave. All day long, our friends came and went. Some were more help than others.

Pamela would not use the hose because she did not want to get sprayed. She would

not use the wax because she did not want to get it on her clothes.

"What *will* you do?" I asked her.

"Count the money," she said. "I will make change for the customers."

So that was Pamela's job.

In the afternoon we had pretty many customers. Once, three cars were lined up waiting, while we washed a fourth car.

"Isn't it a good thing cars get so dirty?" I said to Nancy.

"I'll say," she agreed.

By four o'clock my friends and I were very tired.

"Why don't you close the car wash?" Kristy suggested.

So we did. We closed it even before we knew how much money we had earned. Natalie and Addie counted it while the rest of us cleaned up.

"How much?" I asked Natalie when they were finished.

"Twenty-nine dollars," she replied.

"Twenty-nine. Is that enough?"

"It depends on how much everyone earned yesterday," said Addie.

We would have to wait and see. One good thing: Ms. Colman had not driven by the car wash.

10

Natalie's Job

"Do I really have to go to school?" I asked Mommy. I yawned and rolled over. I did not want to get out of bed.

"You certainly do."

"Yuck." I was tired. I had worked hard all weekend. I pulled the pillow over my head. Then I heard another voice. It was Andrew's.

"Don't you want to find out how much money you earned?" he asked.

"Oh, yeah!" Suddenly I was wide awake. Today was the day we would add up our money. We would find out if we had enough to buy Ms. Colman's present.

After lunch we held a secret meeting on the playground. I took charge.

"Did everybody bring their money?" I asked.

"Yes!"

"The money you earned plus the money you already had?"

"Yes!"

"Natalie, did you bring the money from the car wash, too?"

"Yup," replied Natalie. She was holding a paper bag. She waved it over her head.

"Okay, everybody. Dump out your money," I ordered.

"On the ground?" said Pamela. "It will get dirty."

"Dump it on my tray then," offered Addie. "We can count it there."

One by one, my friends and I stepped up to Addie. We put our money on the tray of her wheelchair. (Addie uses that tray for lots of things. She eats on it in the cafeteria.

She writes on it in our classroom.)

Addie put in her money last of all. Then my classmates and I stared at the pile of bills and coins. We had never seen so much money.

We must have enough for *six* presents," whispered Terri.

"I don't know. What if it looks like more than it really is?" I said. "What if it is not enough?" I bit my lip.

"For heaven's sake. Somebody count it," said Pamela.

"I will do it," said Natalie grandly.

"You be her helper, Addie," I said.

Natalie and Addie began to count the money. I held my breath. I tried to hold it the entire time they were counting, but I could not hold it that long. That is how much money there was.

Natalie and Addie counted and counted. When they finished, they started over. They wanted to be sure they had counted right.

After the second time, Natalie and Addie looked up. They smiled.

"How much?" I asked.

"Sixty-six dollars and seventeen cents," said Addie.

"Yes!" I cried. "Yes, yes, yes!"

And Ricky shouted, "We did it!"

"I think that is enough for the cup and the engraving and the sales tax," said Natalie. "And maybe even for some wrapping paper."

"Now all we have to do is go back to Bellair's and buy the cup," I said.

"I will take care of that," said Natalie. "This was my idea."

"Well . . ." I said.

"It is *my* job," said Natalie firmly. "I will do it today, if Mommy can take me." She scooped the money into the paper bag. "What should we have engraved on the cup?" she asked.

My friends and I thought and thought. Finally we decided on something simple. *To our best teacher: Ms. Colman.*

The bell rang. Recess was over.

"Be careful with the money," Pamela said to Natalie.

"Do not let the bag break," added Bobby.

"Do not *lose* the bag," I said.

"Oh, do not worry," said Natalie. "Everything will be fine."

11

The Big Surprise

I just adore parties. Even if the guests are grown-ups. I like meeting people. I like talking to people. I like eating. I like dancing. That was why I was excited on Friday afternoon. That night Mommy and Seth were giving the party for Ms. Colman and Mr. Simmons. The special party that was also a wedding present. Soon lots of people would be coming to my house.

I had not met many of the people before. Mostly, they were friends of the bride and groom. So I was looking forward to talking to them. I would tell them I was in Ms. Colman's class. I would tell them I was going to be the flower girl. I would tell them about my new dress.

All afternoon Mommy and Andrew and I were very busy. I dusted tables. Andrew emptied wastebaskets. Mommy vacuumed. Andrew and I cleaned up our playroom. Mommy polished silver.

Seth came home early. Then we worked some more. Seth carried platters of food upstairs from the refrigerator in the basement. Mommy set out plates and glasses and knives and spoons and forks and napkins. Andrew and I dumped ice cubes into the ice bucket.

At quarter to five the telephone rang.

"I will get it!" I shouted. I ran for the kitchen.

"Indoor voice, Karen," Mommy said.

"Sorry," I whispered. I picked up the phone. "Hello?" I said.

"Hi, Karen. This is Ms. Colman. May I talk to your mother, please?" Ms. Colman sounded excited. I wondered what was happening.

"Sure," I replied. I handed the phone to Mommy. Then I listened to her end of the conversation. (I thought about picking up the phone in the bedroom and listening to the whole conversation, but I have gotten in trouble with that before. I knew better.)

"Well, that is wonderful!" I heard Mommy say. And then, "How exciting!" (I told you Ms. Colman sounded excited.) And then, "Of course . . . of course. . . . Yes, certainly bring them along. We will just put out a few extra plates. I can't wait to meet them."

When Mommy finally hung up the phone, I pounced on her. "What?" I cried. "What is it? What happened? Who is coming to the party?"

Mommy smiled. "Ms. Colman just got a wonderful surprise," she said. "Guess who rang her doorbell this afternoon."

"Who? Who?" I asked.

"Her sister. Ms. Colman opened her

front door and there were her sister and her sister's husband and Caroline."

"Caroline, her niece?" I squeaked.

"Yes," said Mommy. "They decided to come to the wedding after all. They decided they could not miss it. And they decided they might as well surprise Ms. Colman while they were at it. They are going to stay with her all week, and go home after the wedding. Your teacher is just thrilled, Karen. She is so happy to have her family at the wedding."

A little knot had formed in my stomach. A hard little knot.

I tried to feel excited. Ms. Colman was excited, and Mommy was excited, and now Seth and Andrew looked excited. But I could not feel excited. Instead I felt nervous. And a little scared. I was remembering something about Caroline. Hadn't Ms. Colman said she wanted her niece to be her flower girl? Hadn't she said it was just too bad Caroline lived so far away? That it was too bad she could not come to Stoneybrook and be Ms. Colman's flower girl?

Well, now Caroline was here in Stoneybrook — but Ms. Colman had already asked *me* to be the flower girl. Would she take away my job?

12

Caroline

The knot in my stomach would not go away. I could not stop worrying about Caroline. What was going to happen when Ms. Colman asked her to be the flower girl? Would I have to give her my new dress? Or maybe I would get to keep the dress, but I would just wear it to the wedding. No fair. *I* wanted to be the flower girl. I had been looking forward to that for weeks. No wonder my stomach was tied in a knot. It wasn't very happy.

The knot stayed where it was. It stayed

there while Mommy and Seth and Andrew and I got dressed for the party. It stayed there while Andrew set out coasters and napkins in the living room. It stayed there while Seth arranged a plate of cheese and crackers. It stayed there while Mommy put Rocky and Midgie in Andrew's bedroom. (They were not invited to the party.)

At last we were ready for our guests. The house was ready, the food was ready, my family was ready. We sat in the living room and waited. (We were not allowed to eat anything yet.)

The doorbell rang.

Mommy and Seth answered it. Andrew and I stood behind them.

"Hello!" said Mommy.

"How nice to meet you," said Seth.

Our very first guests were Mr. Simmons, Ms. Colman, Ms. Colman's sister, her husband, and . . . Caroline.

Ms. Colman introduced everybody. "I want you to meet my sister, Pat Bradley," she said. "This is her husband, Doug Brad-

58

ley. And this is their daughter, my niece Caroline. Please meet Lisa and Seth Engle, Andrew Brewer, and Karen Brewer, my flower girl."

Her flower girl? Really? I hoped so, but you never know.

I looked at Caroline. Her dark hair was fixed in two pigtails tied with yellow ribbons. Her eyes were friendly. I thought of Caroline playing the piano and riding horses. I smiled at her. She smiled back.

"Karen," said Mommy, "why don't you show Caroline your room?"

But Caroline did not want to go to my room. She stood back, clinging to her mother's hand. "Not now," she whispered.

So we went into the living room. The doorbell rang again. It rang and rang. The guests arrived in ones and twos and groups. Soon our house was crowded with people. It was party time.

"Let's test the food," I said to Andrew.

We tried the onion dip. We tried some cheese. We shared an anchovy. (Andrew spit his half out.) We tasted some caviar. (I spit mine out.)

Then I introduced myself to every guest. (But I did not say I was the flower girl, just in case.)

Finally Andrew and I grew bored. Caroline looked bored, too. Mommy asked Caroline if she would like to see my room now.

"Okay," said Caroline.

Andrew and I led the way. I showed Caroline my rat. (But Caroline did not want to hold her.) I showed her Goosie and my dolls. I showed her Hyacynthia, the baby doll I share with Nancy.

"Do you like dolls?" I asked Caroline.

"Yes," she whispered.

"Do you like animals?"

"Yes." Caroline smiled. "Especially horses."

"Let's color," I said. We made pictures of our favorite pets. Caroline drew great animals, but she did not talk much.

I decided Caroline was very, very shy.

60

13

Karen's Problem

The party was over. The guests had gone home. I was lying in bed. I was supposed to be sleeping. But I could not sleep. I kept thinking about Caroline. And about the wedding and being the flower girl. I could not stop worrying. I knew Ms. Colman loved her niece. Pictures of Caroline were all over her house. I had seen them myself. Ms. Colman had wanted Caroline to be her flower girl. But Caroline was not going to be able to come to the wedding. So Ms. Colman had asked me to be her flower girl. And now Caroline was here.

I sighed. I rolled over. After a long time I fell asleep.

I thought about Caroline all weekend. I thought about her on Monday when I was back in school. The knot in my stomach did not go away. By Tuesday I had a stomachache.

"Karen?" said Mommy after supper. "Do you feel all right?"

"I guess so," I said. "Well, no. Not really."

"Is anything wrong? You have been very quiet lately."

I drew in my breath. I let it out slowly. Finally I said, "My stomach hurts. I am worried about something. I cannot stop thinking about it."

"What are you worried about?"

"Caroline," I replied. "I think Ms. Colman might ask her to be the flower girl. She wanted Caroline first, remember? She only asked me when she thought Caroline could not come to the wedding."

"But Karen," said Mommy, "Ms. Colman would not have asked you to be her flower girl if she did not really want you. Ms. Colman asked you because she cares about you very much."

"That was before Caroline came," I said. "I think Ms. Colman is going to ask her to be the flower girl instead."

"Don't you remember how Ms. Colman introduced you at the party?" Mommy went on. "She said, 'And this is Karen Brewer, my flower girl.' "

"I know . . ." I replied. But I did not stop worrying.

I will tell you a secret, something I did not even tell Mommy. I thought Caroline really should be the flower girl. And if *I* thought so, then Ms. Colman probably thought so. Caroline had a right to be her aunt's flower girl. But it was supposed to be my job, and I did not want to give it up.

I almost talked to Ms. Colman about the problem, but I just could not do it.

64

14

The Big Mistake

Wednesday went by. Thursday went by. Ms. Colman did not say anything to me about giving my flower girl dress to Caroline. So I guessed I was still going to be the flower girl. But the more I thought about it, the worse I felt. *Caroline* should be the flower girl, yet I did not want to give up the job. I did not know what to do.

On Friday Ms. Colman was absent. But she was not sick. She had told us on Thursday that she would not be in school the next day. This is what she had said: "Boys and girls, tomorrow I will not be here. I will be getting ready for my wedding. I will see you at the wedding on Saturday. After that, I will be on my honeymoon for two weeks. And then I will come back to school."

So on Friday we had a substitute teacher. Her name was Mrs. Hoffman. Mrs. Hoffman had been our substitute before. We did not like her at first. We called her Hatey Hoffman. But now she is our favorite substitute. We were happy to see her. And we were glad she would stay with us during the next two weeks.

"Hi, Mrs. Hoffman!" I cried when Nancy and I ran into our classroom.

"Good morning, Karen," she replied.

"Tomorrow is the wedding!" I said. (I was still excited about the wedding, even if I did not know what to do about Caroline.)

"And I will see you there," said Mrs. Hoffman.

"Oh, goody! You are coming, too."

The other kids were starting to arrive. Hannie and Pamela and Hank and Audrey and the twins and Bobby and Addie and Ricky. We gathered around Mrs. Hoffman.

Then Natalie came into the room. She was holding her lunchbox and a shopping bag. The shopping bag was from Bellair's.

"Ooh, you have the cup!" I exclaimed.

"Yeah," said Natalie.

Natalie looked awful. I think she had been crying. But I was too excited to pay attention to that. "Hey, everyone!" I shouted. "Natalie is here! She has the present for Ms. Colman!"

I was a little surprised, because we had already decided we would give the present to our teacher when she came back to school. Then she could put the cup right on her desk where it belonged. So why had Natalie brought it to school today?

Natalie did not open the bag. She just stood there. Her lip began to tremble.

"What is the matter?" I asked her. "Can we see the cup?"

Natalie handed the bag to me. I peeked inside. I saw a box. I took it out and opened it. Now the kids had gathered around me.

I lifted out the silver cup. It was beautiful. It was more beautiful than I had remembered. And now it was engraved, too. I wondered why Natalie was so upset.

"Ooh," said Pamela and Addie and Audrey.

"It's so pretty," added the twins.

"Read it," said Ricky.

I turned the cup around. I read the inscription. "To our best teacher, Ms. Cotman. . . . Ms. *Cot*man?" I exclaimed.

Natalie nodded. "I did not see the mistake until we had brought the cup home yesterday," she said. "And I think the mistake is all my fault. I wrote down what the man should engrave on the cup. And I am always forgetting and crossing my l's. So we cannot take the cup back, and we do not have any more money for another cup."

"Oh, no!" cried my friends.

"What are we going to do?" I wailed.

Mrs. Hoffman looked thoughtful. "Let's sit down and talk about this," she said.

68

To Our Best

Teacher

Ms. Cotman

15

Karen's Good Idea

That night, the night before my teacher's wedding, I ate dinner someplace very special. I ate it at Ms. Colman's house. Ms. Colman gave a dinner for her relatives who were visiting, for some of her close friends, and for me and my little-house family.

Guess what. The knot in my stomach was gone. Mrs. Hoffman had helped us with our present problem. Plus, I had made a decision about my flower girl problem. I had decided what to do — but I had not told anybody about it yet.

70

Seth drove Mommy and Andrew and me to Ms. Colman's house. He parked the car on the road. A lot of other cars were already there. Andrew and I raced to the porch. I reached it first, and rang the bell.

"I wonder what we will have for supper," I said.

"I hope there won't be any anchovies," Andrew replied.

Ms. Colman heard him. She smiled. "No anchovies," she told us as she opened the door. "I fixed a treat for you two and Caroline."

The treat was pizza. The adults had to eat something with a long funny name. Also, they had to eat in the living room. Andrew and Caroline and I got to eat in the den with the television.

When we had finished our pizza, I said, "Caroline? Could I talk to you for a minute? This is important."

"Okay," said Caroline.

I turned to Andrew. "We need our privacy," I told him.

Andrew decided to see what the grown-ups were having for dessert.

When he was gone, I said, "Caroline, I have been thinking very hard. You should be the flower girl tomorrow. It is only fair. You are Ms. Colman's niece. You should be in her wedding."

Caroline looked startled. Then she looked as if she might cry. "But — but I cannot do that," she said. "Don't *you* want to be the flower girl?"

"Yes," I replied. "Very much. But you should have the job."

"I cannot do that," said Caroline again. "I'm — I'm too shy. I could never walk down the aisle by myself. Everyone would be looking at me. I am *glad* you are the flower girl."

"But you are Ms. Colman's niece," I replied. "Besides, don't you like for people to look at you? I just love it."

Caroline shook her head. "Not me."

"Hmm," I said. And then I got a great

idea. "Caroline!" I cried. "You and I could *both* be flower girls. We could be co-flower girls."

"Well . . ." said Caroline, and she smiled a little.

"We could walk down the aisle side by side," I went on. "Then you would not be alone. You can wear my flower girl outfit if you want. It is brand new. Your aunt helped pick it out, so I know she likes it."

"Oh, that's okay," said Caroline. "Thank you, but I have a new dress, too. I will wear that. You wear your outfit."

"And we will both hold onto the basket of rose petals," I added. "We can scatter the petals at the same time."

"Okay!"

"We better talk to your aunt," I said. "And to Mr. Simmons."

So we did. We found them in the living room. We asked for a private conference in the kitchen. Then we told them about our great idea.

"That sounds lovely," said Ms. Colman. "Co-flower girls."

"A very nice idea," added Mr. Simmons.

Caroline and I looked at each other. We grinned. I felt very proud. I had solved the problem all by myself.

16

Wedding Day

When I woke up the next morning, I thought the knot had returned to my stomach. Then I realized I had butterflies instead. It was wedding day, and I was an intsy bit nervous.

I peeked outside. I saw sunshine and a blue sky.

"Perfect," I said.

I tried to eat breakfast that morning, but it was hard.

"Eat *some*thing," said Seth. "It is a long time until lunch."

So I ate a piece of toast. Then I ran back to my room. I could not wait to get dressed. I put on my underwear. I put on a pair of white tights. I put on the dress and my shoes and the gloves. Then I took off the gloves so I could fix my hair. After that I put the gloves back on, and then the hat. "I'm ready!" I shouted.

Andrew peeked in at me.

"Hey, *you* better get ready," I said to him.

"I am ready."

"You are not." Andrew was wearing his suit. Over his suit he was wearing a plastic tool belt. It was strapped around his waist. A plastic hammer and a plastic wrench and a plastic screwdriver and a pair of plastic pliers were hanging from it. He would not take it off.

Andrew was still wearing the tool belt when we arrived at the church. (The church was not in Stoneybrook. It was in another town.) Seth parked the car and we walked inside. I pretended Andrew belonged to some other family.

76

We had reached the church early. Even so, the guests were already beginning to arrive. I watched them from the back of the church. Since I was going to be in the wedding, I did not have to sit in one of the pews. Seth sat down with Andrew, though. I was glad, because now you could hardly see the tool belt.

I waited in back with Mommy. There was a lot to see. For awhile I watched the guests arrive. I saw Mrs. Hoffman and her husband. I saw Hannie and her parents, and I waved to them. I saw Nancy and her mother, and I waved to them, too. (Mr. Dawes had stayed at home with the baby.) I saw Ricky and Bobby and Addie and Pamela and Natalie and the twins and all their parents.

Then I noticed something else. In a room off the side of the church a photographer was setting up cameras.

"What for?" I asked Mommy.

"Wedding portraits," she answered.

"Hi, Karen!" someone cried.

I turned around. There was Caroline. She looked beautiful. And she was wearing a straw hat and gloves like mine. "Mommy took me shopping early this morning," she said.

I smiled. "We are practically twins," I replied, even though our dresses were not the same at all.

"Are you the flower girls?" asked a man.

Caroline and I looked up. And up and up. (He was very tall.) "Yes," I said.

"Well, I am the wedding photographer. The bride wants me to take your picture. Would you go into that room, please?"

The photographer pointed to the room with the cameras in it. I took Caroline's hand and we walked into it together. Guess who was there. The bridesmaids, the best man, and an usher — and the bride and groom. They looked just like the little people on top of a wedding cake. Mr. Simmons was wearing a tuxedo, and Ms. Colman was wearing a beautiful long white dress and a veil.

The photographer took several pictures of us. (We were the wedding party.) When he finished, I could hear music playing in the church. And Ms. Colman's sister said to us, "It is time to begin."

Kissing the Bride

Dum, dum, da-dum.

Here comes the bride.

The wedding had begun. The guests were seated in the church. The organ was playing. The minister was standing in front. And now Ms. Colman's bridesmaids were walking down the aisle. First one, then the other. Each was carrying a bouquet of flowers, and they were smiling. The guests had turned around to look at them.

"We're next," I whispered to Caroline.

Caroline nodded. She looked very scared.

"Remember, I will be walking right next to you," I said. I held up the basket of rose petals. Caroline took the handle, so we could carry it between us.

"Okay," said Caroline's mommy. "Go ahead, girls."

My heart began to pound. I stepped forward. Caroline was with me. We began to walk slowly down the aisle. At first I forgot to scatter the rose petals, but when I walked by Nancy, she nudged me and whispered, "Petals!"

"Oh, yeah," I said.

I reached into the basket. I sprinkled a handful of petals on the aisle. Caroline did the same. By the time we reached the minister, the aisle behind us was covered with pink petals. And Ms. Colman was gliding down the aisle in her long dress. I thought she looked like a princess. Caroline's daddy was beside her. He was going to give her away.

Caroline and I stood at the front of the church with the bridesmaids. We stood off to one side. On the other side stood Mr. Simmons. He was smiling, and waiting for Ms. Colman to finish walking down the aisle.

Everyone in the church was looking at Ms. Colman. My classmates were looking at her. Mommy and Seth were looking at her. Andrew (with his tool belt) was looking at her. Her mother was looking at her. Some of the guests were crying. They were not crying loudly like Andrew does when he skins his knee or something. They were just sniffling, and dabbing at their eyes and noses with tissues or handkerchiefs. I even saw two men crying.

Caroline's daddy walked the bride all the way to Mr. Simmons. Then he sat in a front pew. Ms. Colman and Mr. Simmons stood before the minister.

The minister began to talk. I think he liked to talk. I did not listen to most of what he said. Instead I looked around the church. I wondered who else had been married in it. I played with the basket Caroline and I had carried down the aisle. (It was empty now.) I watched Andrew pretend to nail his jacket to the pew.

Then I realized that Ms. Colman had just said, "I do."

Then Mr. Simmons said, "I do."

Then the minister said, "You may kiss the bride."

My eyes opened very wide. I had not been sure he would say that. I did not think teachers kissed in public. But Ms. Colman was lifting up her veil, and Mr. Simmons was leaning toward her.

I looked at the guests. Hannie and Nancy were giggling. They had put their hands over their mouths. Mrs. Papadakis was frowning at them. Ricky and Bobby were blushing. Their faces were blotchy and red. Addie, whose wheelchair was parked in an aisle at the end of a pew, had buried her face in her hands. (Andrew was not paying attention, though. He was trying to fix

Mommy's purse with his plastic screw-driver.)

After the kiss, Ms. Colman and Mr. Simmons walked down the aisle together. Caroline and I were right behind them. I found Mommy and Seth, while the guests waited outside for the bride and groom. Someone passed around bags of birdseed, and when the bride and groom came out, we showered them with it.

The wedding was over.

18

Just Married

Ms. Colman and Mr. Simmons laughed. They ducked their heads under the shower of birdseed. Then they ran into a car that was parked in front of the church. (Someone had taped a sign to the back of the car. It said JUST MARRIED.) Ms. Colman waved to us before the car drove off.

I knew where they were going. They were going to a restaurant. That was where the reception would be held. The reception is the party after the wedding. This one would be small. Not too many guests. Just the wedding party, the relatives, and a few close friends. So I would be at the reception but the rest of my classmates would not.

"Good-bye! Good-bye!" I called to Hannie and Nancy.

"Good-bye!" they called back. And Hannie added, "I cannot believe we saw our teacher *kiss* in public!"

I climbed into our car. Mommy drove Seth and Andrew and me to the restaurant. The restaurant was an old stone inn in the countryside. When we walked through the front door, a woman said to us, "Colman party?" When Seth nodded, she said, "Right through there."

We had an entire room to ourselves. It was only for the people who were going to the reception. No one else could eat in it.

Along one side of the room was a buffet table. It was piled with food.

"Oh, goody," said Andrew. "All you can eat. Just like at Chuckie's Happy House. I wonder if we get free sundae coupons, too."

"Andrew, this is *not* Chuckie's Happy House," I hissed.

One half of the room was crowded with tables and chairs. The other half was empty.

"For dancing," I informed Andrew. "Everyone will be dancing this afternoon. Even my teacher. First I saw her kiss. Now I will see her dance."

The room was filling up. The wedding guests wandered around. They talked and laughed. Waiters and waitresses offered us drinks. Andrew and Caroline and I stuck together. We were the only kids.

When Ms. Colman and Mr. Simmons arrived, everyone cheered. And then the party really began. Two waiters stood behind the buffet table and served up plates of food. Three musicians came into the room and began to play grown-up music. Everyone was either eating or dancing. I looked at the food. Then I looked around for Seth.

"May I have this dance?" I asked him.

"Why, certainly," he replied.

I danced with Seth twice. Then I danced with Mommy. Then I danced with Mr. Simmons. I *tried* to dance with Andrew, but his tool belt kept banging against my legs. So I danced with Caroline instead. After four dances, we took a break. We got some food and ate it at one of the tables. Andrew sat with us. We made our own children's table. (Andrew pretended we were at Chuckie's Happy House.)

Just when I was feeling bored, everyone began to clink their spoons against their glasses. The best man held his glass high and made a toast to the bride and groom. He wished them lots of happiness. Then a waiter wheeled a cart into the room. On the cart was the wedding cake. Ms. Colman and Mr. Simmons cut it and ate the first piece. After that, each guest ate a piece, too.

I was feeling very tired by the time Ms. Colman stood on a chair and threw her bouquet over her shoulder. I did not even

try to catch it. Here's the thing. If you catch it, you will be the next person to get married, and I am already married to Ricky Torres. A friend of Ms. Colman's caught the bouquet.

And that was it. The party was over.

Ms. Colman Comes Back

After Ms. Colman threw her bouquet, she and Mr. Simmons went somewhere to change their clothes. Then they said good-bye to their guests, and they drove away. They were on their honeymoon.

The guests started to leave then, too. Caroline and I had to say good-bye to each other. She and her parents were flying back to Oregon that very night.

"Good-bye, Caroline," I said. "I am glad we were co-flower girls."

"Me, too," said Caroline. "Thank you for thinking of that."

"I wonder if we will ever see each other again," I said.

Caroline paused. "We will see each other in the wedding pictures," she replied finally. "That will be fun."

"And we can write to each other," I added.

"Sure. We can be pen pals."

Caroline and I exchanged addresses. Then it was time to leave. Andrew and I slept all the way home in the car.

Two weeks and two days later, I ran happily into my classroom at Stoneybrook Academy. It was Monday morning. But it was not just *any* Monday morning. It was the day Ms. Colman would come back from her honeymoon. I could not wait to see her.

Neither could my classmates. We stood around the room. We felt very impatient.

"Where is she? Where is she?" we kept saying.

And Natalie even said, "What if she does not come back?"

But I said, "Of course she will come back. Natalie, did you bring — "

"Good morning, girls and boys!"

"She's here! It's Ms. Colman!" we cried.

"She did come back!" added Natalie.

We gathered around Ms. Colman's desk.

"How was your honeymoon?" I asked.

"Did you see Niagara Falls?" asked Bobby Gianelli.

Ms. Colman smiled. "Why don't you sit down? Then I will tell you everything," she replied. And she did.

When she finished, I leaned over and poked Natalie. "Now," I whispered.

"Okay." Natalie stood up. She bent over and pulled something out of her desk. It was a present wrapped in silver paper.

She handed it to Ms. Colman. "This is for you," she said. "It is a wedding present, and it is from all of us. Thank you for inviting us to your wedding. We had lots of fun."

Ms. Colman looked surprised. Surprised and happy. "Thank *you*," she said. She unwrapped the present. She lifted the cup out of the box. "Oh, it is beautiful!" she exclaimed. She turned it around. She saw the engraving.

And Natalie said, "Excuse me, Ms. Colman. I have to tell you something. There is a mistake. And it is my fault. The man spelled your name wrong, and we did not have enough money to buy another cup." Natalie explained how she had crossed the l. "But we wanted you to have the cup anyway," she went on. "We earned the money for it ourselves."

I held my breath. What would Ms. Colman say?

"I *love* the cup," she said. "I would not want it to look any different. I like it no matter how my name is spelled. The important thing is that it is from *you*, my students." Ms. Colman paused. "How *did* you earn enough money to buy this cup?" she asked us.

And so we told her about everything — from the secret meetings to the car wash at Hank's house. And then we settled down to work with our favorite teacher.

Dear Karen, Dear Caroline

Dear Karen,

Hi! How are you? It is me, Caroline, your co-flower girl. I hope you still want to be pen pals.

We had fun flying home on the airplane. We got to watch a movie. It was a mystery with a lot of grown-ups in it, but that was okay.

Is my aunt back at school yet?

Love,
Caroline

DEAR CAROLINE,

HI! I AM FINE. HOW ARE YOU? IT IS ME, KAREN, IN CASE YOU DID NOT KNOW. YES, I STILL WANT TO BE PEN PALS. I HOPE YOU DO NOT MIND THAT I HAVE ANOTHER PEN PAL, THOUGH. HER NAME IS MAXIE, AND SHE LIVES IN NEW YORK CITY. SOMEDAY MAYBE I WILL VISIT HER.

YOUR AUNT IS BACK AT SCHOOL. SHE CAME BACK YESTERDAY. WE GAVE HER A PRESENT. SHE TOLD US ABOUT HER HONEYMOON. SHE AND MR. SIMMONS SAW NIAGARA FALLS. DID YOU KNOW THAT PEOPLE HAVE TRIED TO ROLL OVER THOSE WATERFALLS IN WOODEN BARRELS? WHY WOULD ANYONE DO THAT?

LOVE,
KAREN

Dear Karen,

I asked my mother about the people in the barrels, and she said go figure. I guess some things just do not make sense.

I do not mind if you have another pen pal. I have another pen pal too. His name is José and he lives in Miami. I like having lots of pen pals. Besides, why should grown-ups get all the mail?

Guess what. This is good news and bad news. My piano teacher says I play well enough now to be in a recital. But I do not want to be in a recital. I am too shy. What am I going to do?

Help!

Love,
Caroline

Dear Caroline,

I THINK YOU SHOULD BE IN THE RECITAL. I GOT TO PLAY IN A BAND CONCERT AT SCHOOL ONCE. AND I HAVE BEEN IN SOME PLAYS. I KNOW YOU DO NOT LIKE FOR PEOPLE TO LOOK AT YOU, BUT MAYBE YOU COULD IGNORE THEM. COULD YOU PRETEND THE AUDIENCE IS NOT THERE? YOU SHOULD BE GLAD YOUR TEACHER WANTS YOU TO BE IN THE RECITAL.

LOVE,
KAREN

Dear Karen,
  I guess I could try to ignore the audience. I will let you know what happens.
                    Love,
                    Caroline

DEAR CAROLINE,
GOOD LUCK!   LOVE,
                              KAREN

Dear Karen,
  I did it! I played my piece and I ignored everybody (until the end when they clapped). I was only a little scared. I could do it again if I had to.
        Thank you, and lots of love,
                    Caroline

DEAR CAROLINE,
  Congratuli Congri Congar GOOD FOR YOU!
I KNEW YOU COULD DO IT.

                    xxxooo,
                    KAREN

P.S. YOUR AUNT SAYS HI.

About the Author

ANN M. MARTIN lives in New York City and loves animals. Her cat, Mouse, knows how to take the phone off the hook.

Other books by Ann M. Martin that you might enjoy are *Stage Fright, Me and Katie (the Pest)*, and the books in *The Baby-sitters Club* series.

Ann likes ice cream, the beach, and *I Love Lucy*. And she has her own little sister, whose name is Jane.

Little Sister

Don't miss #40

KAREN'S NEWSPAPER

Charlie was the first to call.

"Karen?" he said when I had picked up the phone. "I just want to say thanks. Thanks a whole lot." Charlie did not sound thankful at all. He sounded angry.

"Um, what for?" I asked.

"I just read *The 3M Gazette.* Who said you could write an article about that bracelet and my girlfriend? And how did you find out how much the bracelet cost? I did not tell you any of those things."

"Well . . ." I began.

"You had no right," Charlie went on. "That is my private business. I do not want people to know I am trying to impress Ellen. Sam has been laughing at me all evening. I hope Ellen does not see your paper."

Oops. I had not thought about that.

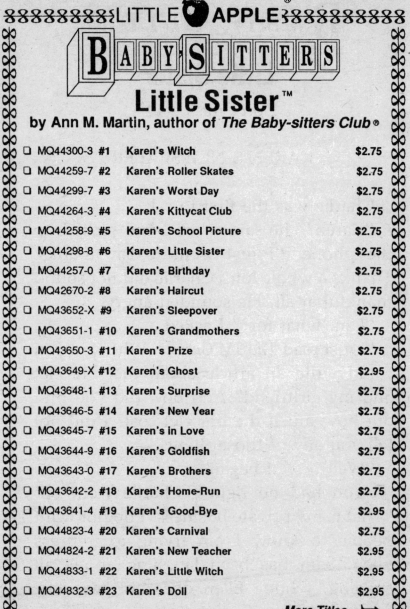